ROBERT BARRY

HOUGHTON MIFFLIN COMPANY BOSTON / THE RIVERSIDE PRESS CAMBRIDGE

1959

This is the story of B O O.

BOO lived on Farmer Brown's farm
with six prize cows,
eleven French hens
and Mrs. Farmer Brown.

The farm was an exciting place for B O O.

There seemed to be all sorts of things to do.

B O O was especially fond of kicking.

MOOO

MOO

MOO

MOO

She was called **B O O** because she had never
quite learned how to say **M O O**
the way that the prize cows could.

BOO

BOO was not like the other cows.
She liked to toast herself
in the warm summer sunshine.

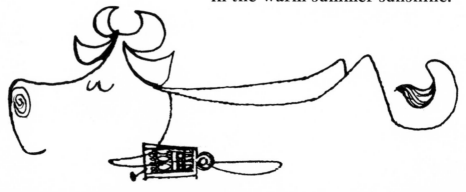

She liked to sit in Farmer Brown's cornfield
and admire the fat ears of corn.

And most of all,
she liked to explore
the nooks and corners
of the pasture
looking for candytuft

and sweet persimmon
leaves.

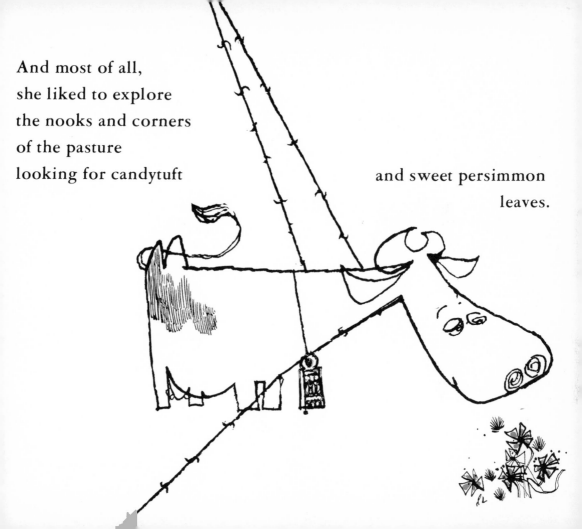

At the end of every day, the prize cows
would come home wagging their tails
and MOOing their happy MOOs.

BOO, however, hardly ever came home on time.
She would rather linger in the quiet fields,
humming her favorite tunes and singing her favorite songs.
One that she especially liked and that she
had composed herself went something like this:

B-BOO B-B-BOO BOO B-BOO BOO BOO.

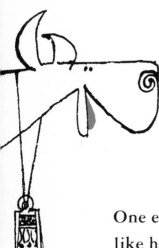

One evening when BOO didn't feel very much
like humming or singing, she came home early.
There was great excitement around the farm.
The COUNTY FAIR was coming!
This might mean more prizes for the prize cows.
BOO was very excited.

COUNTY
FAIR
PRIZES
BLUE
BLUE
RIBBONS

She was so excited, in fact,
that she stood in line with the other cows
to be dressed for the fair.

21

And she WAS dressed for the fair,

with a beautiful bouquet of . . .

CANDYTUFT AND SWEET PERSIMMON LEAVES.

Before Farmer Brown could turn around twice,
BOO had EATEN every bit of it!

Well, someone had to stay at home
with **Mrs. Farmer Brown**
and the eleven French hens.

THAT NIGHT

while Farmer Brown was away at the fair . . .

there was a mysterious visitor in the barn.
He was scooping up the French hens
and slipping them into his sack
just as though they belonged there
in the first place.

As the eleventh French hen disappeared
into the sack, B O O decided that this stranger
was apparently up to no good.

Now, she couldn't say Hello or
How do you do or anything like that,
but she could say BOO...

was the loudest, and the longest, and the
noisiest BOO that anyone had ever said!
At the same time, BOO gave the stranger
one of her very best kicks.

33

The stranger, needless to say,
had never been so frightened. He jumped
and ran just as far as he could,
never stopping once to think about all
the French hens he had left behind.

Of course, as soon as Farmer Brown came home
Mrs. Farmer Brown told him how B O O had saved her
and the eleven French hens
from the terrible chicken thief.

This made Farmer Brown very happy.

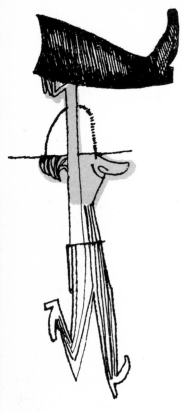

As a special reward for B O O, he brought her all kinds of interesting things to kick.

After that, the prize cows thought that
they should learn how to kick, too.

And some of them thought
it would be a good idea
if they could say BOO instead of MOO.

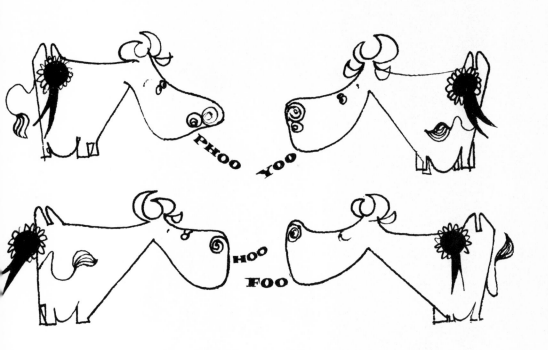

One of them learned to say PHOO
and another learned to say HOO.

But none of them learned to say BOO
the way BOO could.